This book is dedicated to Mom,
and to my fond memories
of Grandma Nault.

AMANDA
and the Witch Switch

John Himmelman

Picture
Ladybird

Up in the hills…

deep in the forest…

there lived a friendly old witch.
Her name was Amanda.

One morning while she was rocking in
her chair, she decided it was too lovely a
day to spend indoors.

Amanda stepped outside and stretched.
"What a beautiful day it is," she said.
"Today I will do something extra nice!"

She added some flowers here and there...

taught some beavers how to boogie...

and some trees how to sing...

but that still didn't seem like enough.

Then she came upon a little toad sitting on a rock.

"My name is Amanda," she said, "and it is such a nice day today that I will make three of your wishes come true."

"Okay," said the toad. "Make me
a prince."

"Sorry, I can only do that for frogs,"
she answered.

"All right then," said the toad. "Make me a witch, like yourself."

Amanda thought for a moment. "Well, I suppose I could," and...

POOF!

The toad turned into a witch!

Then the toad pointed to Amanda.
"And now I want *you* to turn into a toad."

And... *POOF!*
Amanda was turned into a toad.

Amanda sat there *looking* helpless as
the toad went off into the forest.

"Now I can do any magic I want,"
he said.

He turned a pond into mud…

made a deer's antlers into flowers…

turned some rocks into marshmallows...

and made some rabbits turn purple.

He made a bear the size of a bee…

and a bee the size of a bear.

But this last prank backfired,
and the bee went after the toad!

"I'll just turn myself back into a toad
and threaten to eat him if he doesn't
put me down," he thought.

But this didn't quite work out the way he planned.

"*Help*," he called to Amanda. "*Please help me!*"

"I guess he's learned his lesson," thought Amanda, and she turned the bee back to normal size.

"Well, you still have one more wish,"
she said to the toad.

"I wish everything was back the way it was," he said.

"I thought you would," said Amanda, and she turned everything back to normal.

Well, almost everything.